Well, Really, Mr Twiddle!

Text illustrations by Stephen Dell
Cover illustration by Lesley Smith

AWARD PUBLICATIONS LIMITED

Enid Blyton's Happy Days!

Snowball the Pony

Bimbo and Topsy

Run-About's Holiday

The Adventures of Binkle and Flip

Binkle and Flip Misbehave

Mister Meddle's Mischief

Mister Meddle's Muddles

Merry Mister Meddle

You're a Nuisance Mister Meddle

Collect all the titles in the series!

Enid Blyton

The Adventures of
Mr Pink-Whistle

Mr Pink-Whistle
Has Some Fun

Mr Pink-Whistle's
Party

Mr Pink-Whistle
Interferes

Hello
Mr Twiddle!

Mr Twiddle
in Trouble Again

Don't Be Silly,
Mr Twiddle!

Mr Twiddle
in Trouble Again

Shuffle
the Shoemaker

For further information on Enid Blyton please visit *www.blyton.com*

ISBN 978-1-84135-660-0

Illustrations copyright © Award Publications Limited

First published 1953 by George Newnes

First published by Award Publications Limited 2004
This edition first published 2010

Published by Award Publications Limited,
The Old Riding School, The Welbeck Estate,
Worksop, Nottinghamshire, S80 3LR

11 2

Printed in the United Kingdom

Contents

Chapter 1

Well, Really, Mr Twiddle!

'I'm certainly in luck today,' said Mr Twiddle, looking very pleased with himself. 'First, I found that nice pencil I lost last week, and then when I went to feed the hens there were five eggs, and now the postman has brought me a present from my sister Hannah – a nice new hat!'

He tried it on. It certainly was a nice hat. Mrs Twiddle wanted to put a little brown hen feather in the band, but Mr Twiddle wouldn't let her.

'No. I don't like feathers in hats,' he said. 'If only I had a nice new suit now, to go with my hat. I *should* look smart!'

'Well, as you're having such a lucky day you might find one lying in the road,' said Mrs

Twiddle, with a giggle.

'You simply never know what might happen when your luck is in,' said Twiddle. 'I wouldn't be a bit surprised if I found a five-pound note when I was out walking this morning.'

'Well, you'd have to take it to the police station and hand it in to the police, and tell them to find the owner,' said Mrs Twiddle.

'Ah, but as my luck is in they wouldn't find the owner, and they would have to give it back to me,' said Mr Twiddle, still admiring himself in his new hat.

'You've got it on back to front, but I suppose you don't really mind that,' said Mrs Twiddle, with another little giggle.

A timid knock came at the door, and a little girl's head peeped in. 'Please, Mrs Twiddle, may I borrow your cat to play with this morning?'

'Certainly, dear,' said Mrs Twiddle. 'Call her. She does so love playing with a kind little girl like you.'

Mr Twiddle watched the little girl carry the purring cat away, and he looked very pleased. 'Well, if that isn't *another* bit of luck!' he said. 'We've got rid of that cat for a whole morning. Now I can walk about the house without falling over it.'

'I don't know why you don't like our dear old cat,' said Mrs Twiddle. 'You're the only person who ever falls over it, anyway.'

'And do you know why?' said Mr Twiddle, suddenly looking rather fierce. 'I'll tell you! It's because I'm the only person that cat tries to trip up! She's always walking through my legs! Bit of good luck, I tell you, Puss going off with Polly.'

'Well, if you don't go and get the fish for dinner your good luck will come to an end, because you'll go hungry,' said Mrs Twiddle, looking at the clock. 'Put on your old hat, Twiddle, and get the shopping basket, do. Take some paper with you for the fish.'

Twiddle fetched the basket. He put a newspaper in it to wrap the fish in when he bought it. But he didn't change his nice new hat for his old one. No, he thought he looked so nice in the new one that he felt he might as well give everyone a treat when they looked at him!

'Put your *old* hat on!' called Mrs Twiddle, when she saw him going out with his new one on his head.

'No, no, dear,' said Mr Twiddle, trying to find a quick reason for keeping it on. 'I told you my luck is in today – suppose I find a nice new suit somewhere. I'd look dreadful if I didn't have a nice hat to wear with it.'

'Don't be silly, Twiddle!' called his wife, but by that time he was out of the front gate and couldn't hear her. He hurried along to the fish shop.

He stood in the queue for ten minutes and then got a large piece of rather smelly cod.

He had it wrapped carefully in the newspaper, and hoped that he wouldn't be followed home by half a dozen cats.

'I won't go home through the village in case the cats smell the fish and come after me,' thought Twiddle, remembering how annoyed he had been last time by having five cats trailing after him all the way home, sniffing the kippers in his basket. 'I'll go back through the wood.'

So he took the other way home and wandered along in the wood, enjoying the smell of the hawthorn blossom and the sight of the bluebells. It was a very hot day, and Mr Twiddle was glad he hadn't got an overcoat on.

Then he saw a most extraordinary sight. He stopped and looked as if he couldn't believe his eyes. Neatly folded up under a bush was a suit of beautiful new clothes!

Twiddle stood and stared and his heart began to thump in excitement. There! What had he said that very morning! His luck was certainly in, because here was a new suit of clothes waiting to go with his nice new hat!

'But, wait, Twiddle,' said Twiddle to himself, cautiously. 'They might belong to

11

someone, you know. Have a look around and see.'

So he had a good look round, but he could see nobody at all. He went back to the neat pile of clothes and looked at them. Coat, trousers, waistcoat, vest, socks, braces – why, there was everything except a hat!

'This is most extraordinary,' said Twiddle. 'It just shows what can happen when your luck is in! I get a new hat from Hannah – and, lo and behold, I find a complete set of new clothes to go with it, and nobody to own them!'

He looked at them again. They were exactly his size. They were *meant* for him! He looked at the collar of the suit, half expecting to see his own name marked there, and was quite disappointed when it wasn't. But, would you believe it, on the neat white handkerchief folded inside the left-hand top pocket of the coat was the letter T in pale blue thread! Twiddle stared in the greatest delight.

'That proves it,' he said. 'Absolutely. Completely. No doubt whatever. This certainly is my lucky morning! Goodness knows what I shall find next!'

He picked up the clothes and was about to put them into his basket when he remembered the fish. 'Better undo the fish, take a bit of the paper and wrap up the clothes in it or they'll smell of fish,' said Twiddle, forgetting that the paper must smell very strongly of fish already.

He wrapped the clothes up carefully in some of the newspaper, and then made his way home, wondering what bit of good luck would happen to him next. 'I shall put on this new suit as soon as I get home,' thought Mr Twiddle, 'and wear it with my new hat. How grand I shall look.'

He was longing to tell his wife of his new piece of luck, and he was disappointed when he got home and found that she was out. He went to get himself some lemonade to drink, and then heard Mrs Twiddle at the front door. She was talking to somebody.

'Bother! She's brought a visitor home,' thought Mr Twiddle, who didn't like his wife's visitors very much because they talked such a lot.

Then he got a terrible shock. Mrs Twiddle brought her visitor into the kitchen, and Twiddle could hardly believe his eyes when he saw a poor shivering, dripping man in a wet swim-suit! He gaped at him in surprise.

'Twiddle! I met this poor fellow running down the street in an awful state,' said Mrs Twiddle. 'He thought he would bathe in the Blue Pool because it was so hot today, so he took his swim-suit and went to the wood. He took off his nice new clothes, hid them under a bush, and went to bathe.'

'And w-w-when I c-c-c-came b-b-b-back, they had been t-t-taken by a r-r-robber!' said the shivering man, standing as close to the kitchen fire as he could.

'So, Twiddle, I brought the poor fellow in

here, and I thought you could lend him a suit,' said Mrs Twiddle, 'and I thought I'd give him a good hot meal, or he'll get a terrible cold, and then perhaps you'd go along to the police station with him and tell the police about the robbery. I mean, a man who is hateful enough to take a bather's clothes deserves to go to prison at once!'

Twiddle's heart went right down into his boots and stayed there. He stared at his wife in such a peculiar way that she thought he must be ill. He couldn't say a single word.

But he thought a lot! 'Oh, dear! So they were *his* clothes – and he was bathing! Why didn't I think of the Blue Pool? Oh, dear, oh, dear – I hope Mrs Twiddle doesn't look in the basket yet and find the clothes. What am I to *do*?'

Twiddle, don't stand there gaping like a moonstruck goldfish!' said Mrs Twiddle, sharply. 'Go and get an old suit of clothes, quickly. Do you want this poor fellow to die of cold?'

Mr Twiddle wasn't sure if he did or not, he felt in such a terrible muddle. He went upstairs to think it over, but then came down again very quickly when he remembered he had left the basket in the scullery with the fish and the suit there. He must certainly hide that basket!

He snatched up the basket, opened the scullery window and dropped the basket and its contents neatly outside under a lilac bush. There! They would be safe there till he could think what was best to do.

'Twiddle! What in the world are you doing in the scullery?' called his wife. 'You don't keep your clothes *there*! They're in the cupboard upstairs.'

Twiddle shot upstairs. He sank down on his bed. What could he do? What could he say? Nobody would believe him if he said he had thought that finding those clothes was just a bit of the good luck he had had that day. He could see himself now that it had been a very silly thing to think. But he really had thought it.

'If I go down and give him his right clothes, he might quite well haul me off to the police station and put me into prison,' thought poor Mr Twiddle. 'And if I don't give him them I shall feel really awful. He's got to have them back somehow.

Mrs Twiddle shouted upstairs: 'TWIDDLE!

Will you bring some clothes down at once for this poor shivering fellow? I'm just going to cook dinner quickly, so that he can have something hot. Where's the fish?'

Now Twiddle was in another muddle. The fish was in the basket underneath the lilac bush outside the scullery window. But he couldn't say that, of course. He seemed to be getting deeper and deeper into trouble. He scrabbled hastily in the cupboard and took down an armful of clothes. Mrs Twiddle gave them to the wet, shivering bather, and shut him into the sitting-room to change.

'Where's the fish?' she said to Twiddle, sharply.

'Er – now let me see,' said Twiddle looking very vague. 'Now – just let me see.'

A miaow suddenly came from the scullery next to the kitchen. 'There's Puss back again,' said Mrs Twiddle, and she looked pleased. 'Open the kitchen door and let her in, Twiddle. She's a real home-cat – never stays away for long!'

Twiddle opened the door, feeling that his good luck had completely vanished. The cat appeared, dragging behind it a pair of fishy-smelling trousers!

17

Twiddle stared at the cat with great dislike.
He knew at once what had happened. That
tiresome animal had come home, smelt the
fish in the basket lying under the clothes, and
had scrabbled about in the paper and
brought in the trousers, because they now
smelt so deliciously of fish.

'Well! Look at that!' said Mrs Twiddle, in
the greatest astonishment. 'Whatever will the
cat bring in next? A pair of trousers! Where
did she get them from?'

The cat disappeared, and came back again
dragging a coat, which also smelt very

strongly of fish. Mrs Twiddle began to think she must be in some kind of peculiar dream made up of shivering bathers, fishy clothes and a cat that came in and out with them.

Then the sitting-room door flew open and out came the bather, looking very different in Twiddle's old suit, which fitted him perfectly. He stood still and stared when he saw his coat and trousers over Mrs Twiddle's arm – and then stared even more when the cat reappeared, dragging a pair of fishy socks.

'I say – look – they're my clothes the cat is bringing in,' stammered the man, in amazement.

'*Your* clothes? Your c-c-c –' stammered Mrs Twiddle, thinking that her dream was turning into a nightmare. 'But how could Puss find them? Oh, goodness me, now she's bringing in a vest!'

The man picked up all his clothes. Mr Twiddle forced himself to speak in an ordinary kind of voice, though he was trembling inside. 'Well – if they're your clothes, perhaps you'd like to go back into the sitting-room again, take off my suit, and put your own on.'

'No,' said the man, decidedly, sniffing at

his clothes. 'They smell of fish. I couldn't possibly wear them till the smell is gone. If you don't mind, I'll wear yours till tomorrow, then put my own on, I'll return yours then. I'll go now – but I wish I knew where your cat got my clothes from.'

He went out of the front door and banged it shut. Mrs Twiddle stared at Mr Twiddle, feeling rather faint. She sat down in her rocking-chair. 'Oh, Twiddle! I don't understand this at all. I feel quite strange. How did Puss get those clothes? Do you think she was clever enough to understand all we said, and went to hunt for them and found them?'

'No, I don't,' said Twiddle. 'It was just a bit of that cat's usual interference. She –'

Mrs Twiddle alarmed him by suddenly leaping to her feet with a yell. 'Look! The cat's got the fish! Is that the fish you brought home for dinner, Twiddle? Oh, she's stolen it – she's over the wall by now. Twiddle, where did you put that fish, you silly, stupid fellow?'

'It was in the basket – er – under the lilac bush,' said poor Twiddle.

Mrs Twiddle looked at him as if he was quite mad. 'Under the lilac bush! But WHY? Have you gone mad, Twiddle? You'd better go to bed, I think. You must be ill.'

Twiddle thought that bed would be a very nice peaceful place, and he went up very thankfully. There was no dinner because the cat had taken the fish, but Mr Twiddle didn't mind that. It was nice to be able to pretend to be asleep, and not be asked any more awkward questions. *What* a good thing the cat had found the clothes and brought them in, after all! Now nobody would ever know the silly thing he had done in taking them home himself.

But Twiddle is going to get a shock – because that bather isn't going to come back with Twiddle's old suit! He's a dishonest fellow, and he's going to keep it. But how can Twiddle go to the police and complain about *that*? Didn't he do exactly the same thing himself, when he thought his luck was in?

Poor old Twiddle! He's not so lucky, after all!

Chapter 2

Mr Twiddle Forgets

'Twiddle, it's the New Year tomorrow,' said Mrs Twiddle, busily darning an enormous hole in one of Mr Twiddle's socks. 'New Year's Eve tonight – the time when people make good resolutions.'

'What exactly is a resolution?' asked Mr Twiddle. 'It's such a long and peculiar word.'

'Well – when you make a resolution it just means that you resolve to do something and really mean it,' said Mrs Twiddle. 'Don't pretend you don't know that, Twiddle! You make a promise to yourself – you determine to do something; but if you make this resolution on New Year's Eve it's very important and very special.'

'Oh!' said Twiddle. 'Have *you* made any good resolutions?'

'Dear me, yes,' said Mrs Twiddle. 'I've resolved not to be cross with the paper-boy when he brings the wrong paper – and I've resolved to mend all those old shirts of yours I've been putting off for so long – and I've resolved not to let you snore at nights –'

'Well! What a peculiar resolution!' said Mr Twiddle, indignantly. 'Surely that ought to be *my* resolution, not yours?'

'Oh, no, dear – because *you* can't stop yourself snoring, and I very well can,' said Mrs Twiddle. 'I've only got to pinch you hard and you stop.'

'Well, I don't think that's at all a nice resolution to make,' said Twiddle.

'Now, now, don't be silly. You think about your own resolutions, not mine,' said Mrs Twiddle.

Twiddle thought, 'I've got quite a lot in my mind,' he said at last. 'I'll remember to chop the wood for you. I'll remember to mend that chair leg you've been asking me about for ages. I'll resolve to be kinder to the cat – though that will be hard because she honestly does try to trip me up on purpose, I'm sure of it – still, I'll buy her some fish to show her I mean to be kind.'

'Miaow,' said the cat, thrilled, and dug its claws into Twiddle's ankles as it stretched itself.

'What do you want to do that for, you unkind, horrible creature?' shouted Twiddle, and scolded the cat.

'Well!' said Mrs Twiddle, in surprise. 'I don't think much of your resolutions if you forget them so quickly.'

'I haven't forgotten,' said Twiddle. 'But I haven't begun them yet – it isn't New Year's Day till tomorrow. Now, let me think – I'll make a resolution to wind up the clock – and to paint the shed – and to sweep the kitchen chimney for you – and –'

'Now, Twiddle, it's not a good thing to make so many resolutions,' said Mrs Twiddle. 'Make *one* – one good sensible one – and keep it.'

'All right,' said Twiddle, 'I will. I know! I'll make a resolution not to forget a single thing! There – now you won't have to keep on telling me what a dreadful memory I have.'

'Splendid!' said Mrs Twiddle. 'Now you write down that resolution and put it somewhere to remind you – or else you'll forget it.'

So Twiddle wrote out his resolution in his best handwriting. 'My New Year's Resolution is that I will not forget a single thing!'

He stood it behind the clock where he could see it. He felt very pleased with himself. Aha! He would show Mrs Twiddle that he could make just as good resolutions as she could!

Next morning he heard his wife up very early. He called down in astonishment to know why she was up.

'Oh, just one of my good resolutions,' said Mrs Twiddle. 'I've determined I will never be late down in the morning. I hope you've remembered *your* resolution, Twiddle.'

Twiddle lay back in bed and thought hard. Now, what *was* his resolution? What could it have been? To be kind to the cat and get her fish? To wind up the clock? To mend something? Now *what* was that fine, sensible resolution he had made?

He fell asleep trying to remember. It was no use, he just couldn't think of it. He was very late down for breakfast and Mrs Twiddle was cross.

'Late the first morning of the year! And what about that good resolution of yours? Have you remembered it?'

Well, Mrs Twiddle was in one of her rather bustling moods, and Twiddle simply didn't dare to tell her he had already forgotten what his good resolution was. 'You just wait and see,' he told Mrs Twiddle.

After breakfast he tried again to remember what he had resolved to do. 'Was it to chop the wood?' he wondered. 'Perhaps it was. I'll do it.'

So out he went and chopped a whole lot of wood for Mrs Twiddle. She was very pleased. But Twiddle didn't feel that had been his resolution. He tried something else. He stroked the cat and then actually went out to buy it some fish. But no – surely that wasn't his resolution? Mrs Twiddle didn't say anything to make him think it was.

Twiddle found the broken chair and mended the leg.

Now, surely *that* had been his resolution? Mrs Twiddle thanked him heartily. But she didn't say it was nice to see he had kept his resolution. So it couldn't be that.

Poor Twiddle! The things he did that day to try and find out what it was he had made a resolution about! He swept both the kitchen and the sitting-room chimneys and covered himself with soot. He had to have a bath, and he actually remembered to clean it after him – but somehow he didn't feel that had anything to do with his resolution either.

'I believe it was to paint the shed!' thought Mr Twiddle, and out he went to get a tin of paint and a brush.

Mrs Twiddle came out to watch. 'Well, you really are good today,' she said. 'And how well you've painted the shed. Anyone would think you had made a good resolution to do it today!'

Oh, dear! So he hadn't made a resolution about painting the shed. Mr Twiddle felt very gloomy. How many more things was he going to do before he remembered what his resolution really was! If only he could ask Mrs Twiddle what it was. But she would laugh at him too much. No, he really must remember it himself.

He went in to wash for tea, wondering what else there was for him to do.

Wind up the clock! Yes, of course – perhaps

that was his good resolution. Twiddle went to the clock on the mantelpiece and hunted for the key. Mrs Twiddle looked up.

'Reading your good resolution again?' she said.

'What do you mean?' asked Twiddle – and then he suddenly saw the good resolution he had written out so neatly the night before, and stood behind the clock. There it was, staring him in the face – 'My New Year's Resolution is that I will not forget a single thing!'

So that was it – dear, dear! – and the first thing he had done was to forget what his resolution had been! Whatever would Mrs Twiddle say if she knew?

'You've remembered your resolution marvellously, I think,' she said. 'Really marvellously! You haven't forgotten a single thing all day long, Twiddle. I do feel so pleased. I shall cook you a very special kipper for your tea!'

He did enjoy his kipper – but, you know, he didn't say a word to Mrs Twiddle about forgetting his resolution – not one single word. It's still there, behind the clock. I wonder how soon he'll forget it again!

Chapter 3

Twiddle Cuts the Grass

'I do wish,' said Mrs Twiddle, 'I *do* wish, Twiddle, that you would do something about that long grass in the garden. It looks so very untidy.'

Mrs Twiddle said this almost every day. Mr Twiddle sighed. He knew he would have to cut that grass sooner or later. Well, it was a nice day. He might as well do it and get it over.

'Very well, my love,' he said. 'I'll take the scythe and mow it down. Anything to please you!'

'Well, put your garden trousers on, dear,' said Mrs Twiddle. 'You don't want to spoil your nice ones.'

Twiddle went upstairs and found his

garden trousers. They were old, grey flannel ones and he liked them. They were big and comfortable.

He put them on and then took everything out of the pockets of his other trousers and put them into the pockets of his garden trousers. In went his money, his keys, his handkerchief and a little roll of string that he always kept in case he might want some.

Then he went downstairs to find the scythe. 'It may be blunt, of course,' he said to Mrs Twiddle. 'Then I couldn't start mowing the grass today.'

'Well, it isn't blunt,' said Mrs Twiddle. 'I had it sharpened last week for you. Now do get to work, Twiddle – you've been ages already getting your garden trousers on.'

Twiddle went out into the garden. It was rather hot. Oh dear, scything was very very hard work! He would soon be dreadfully hot! He took off his coat.

He walked to the long grass with the big scythe in his hand. Dear, dear, it certainly was very long! He felt the blade of the scythe to see if it really was sharp, and it was.

Now, just as Mr Twiddle was about to begin his work, the cat walked over to him, and rubbed against his leg in a very loving manner. Twiddle was not very fond of his wife's cat. It always wanted doors or windows opened for it whenever Twiddle was sitting down reading his paper.

'Go away, Puss!' he said, sternly. 'I'm going to do a bit of scything. You don't want your tail cut off, do you? Well, use your brains, then, and get away. Shoo!'

The cat rubbed itself against Mr Twiddle's other leg. Then it sat down and began to wash itself.

'Did you hear what I said?' asked Twiddle.

'Go away from this long grass. Right away. Surely you would not be silly enough to lie down and sleep in it just when I'm going to scythe it? Of course, I know that's just the kind of thing you *would* do!'

The cat immediately curled itself up in the grass and tucked its head into its paws. Twiddle stirred it with his foot.

'Now, what did I say? Go and find Mrs Twiddle! Go along!'

The cat uncurled itself, went a little way away, gave Twiddle a nasty look and settled down again. Mr Twiddle began to get angry. He ran at the cat.

'Shoo! Get away! Why do you always make things difficult for me?'

The cat decided that Twiddle wanted to have a game with it. It jumped up, crouched down, and ran at Twiddle's feet. Then it darted away into the grass and hid. Twiddle ran at it again. 'Shoo! *Will* you go away and let me get on with my work?'

Mrs Twiddle put her head out of the window. 'Twiddle! What are you doing rushing about in the grass all by yourself and shouting like that?'

'I'm *not* all by myself!' shouted back

Twiddle, indignantly. 'The cat's here. How can I cut the grass if she's darting about the whole time?'

He chased the cat all about the grass and at last it ran off to Mrs Twiddle, its tail straight up in the air. Twiddle, feeling very hot, panted a bit, and then lifted the scythe.

But just as he was about to begin his work he saw something lying in the grass, something bright and round. He picked it up. A ten pence! Well, that was a nice little find. Very nice, indeed. He put it into his pocket with his other money.

'It's a pity I can't find a bit more money,' he said to himself. 'If I could I'd pay a man to do this heavy scything.'

He cut a piece of grass – and then he suddenly saw something shining once more. He bent down – goodness gracious, it was twenty pence!

'Very strange!' said Mr Twiddle. 'Someone's been walking in this grass, I suppose, and dropped a bit of money. Who's been trespassing in my garden? Well, it serves him right to lose his money!'

He lifted his scythe again, and then thought that he might as well have a look to see if there was any more money lying in the long grass. So he put down his scythe and began to look.

He soon saw five pence and two pence! Then he found another ten pence. Well, well, this *was* a nice surprise, to be sure! 'Forty-seven pence altogether. Splendid!'

He began to look very carefully indeed, bending down and peering in the grass, parting the long blades hopefully.

'Another twenty pence! Well, I never! And here's fifty pence. Would you believe it! Why, this bit of grass is full of money!'

It was most extraordinary. He kept on picking up five pences and two pences, ten pences and twenty pences wherever he looked. He put them all into his pocket, feeling very pleased indeed. 'I shall get a man to come and do the scything now. Why, I must have picked up about a five pound's worth of money already. Very nice, very nice indeed!'

Mrs Twiddle looked out of the window again to see if Twiddle was getting on well with his scything. She saw him bending down, creeping here and there, then suddenly standing up to put something into his pocket, then bending down again and creeping about. What *was* he doing?

'Twiddle!' shouted Mrs Twiddle. 'What *do* you think you're doing? Surely you're not playing with the cat?

'I am not!' said Twiddle, standing up, looking rather hot. 'I'm picking up money.'

'Good gracious!' said Mrs Twiddle. 'Money! Whatever do you mean?'

'What I say,' said Twiddle, and bent down to pick up a ten pence. He held it up to show her. 'It's easy. I just look for it and I see it. It's all over this piece of grass. Wherever I go I find five pences and two pences and ten pences and twenty pences and fifty pences. Why, here's fifty pence by my foot now!'

So there was. Mrs Twiddle hurried down to the patch of long grass. 'Really, Twiddle! I can't believe it. How could there be so much money in this grass? Where in the world did it come from?'

'Somebody must have dropped it,' said Twiddle. 'Somebody trespassing in my garden. Serves him right to lose it.'

He picked up a ten pence and put it into his pocket. 'I'm going to pay a man to do this scything instead of me,' he said. 'And if you'd like to buy yourself a box of chocolates, I'd be pleased to give you the money. And we might perhaps buy a chicken for our dinner.'

Mrs Twiddle looked very puzzled. She couldn't understand this money business at all. Twiddle wandered away a little and then picked up a five pence. 'See! I tell you wherever I go in this grass I pick up money.'

'Your pocket must be absolutely full of it!' said Mrs Twiddle. 'How much have you got?'

'Well, I've picked up dozens and dozens of five pences and ten pences and twenty pences and things,' said Twiddle. 'I'll show you what I've got.'

He put his hand into his pocket to get out all the money he had put there. He felt round his pocket and a frown came on his face.

'What's the matter?' said Mrs Twiddle.

'A most extraordinary thing,' said Twiddle, looking astonished, 'I can't feel even a five pence in my pocket! And yet I put dozens of coins there. Where have they all gone?'

'Let me feel,' said Mrs Twiddle, and she put her hand into his pocket. She felt around – and then she found a big hole at the bottom!

'Twiddle! You've got an enormous hole in that pocket. I really do think you are the stupidest man I've ever known! Here you go walking about with a hole in your pocket, dropping all your money out, and picking it up and putting it in your pocket again and then out it falls, and you pick it up all over again – and think you're so rich we can have chicken for dinner!'

Mr Twiddle stared at his wife in dismay. He felt the hole in his pocket. 'Have I – have I been picking up the same five pence and the same ten pence, and the same twenty pence all the time?' he said. 'Wasn't this grass full of money, then?'

'No, you stupid man! Whatever money was

here fell from your pocket – when you were chasing the cat about, I should think,' said Mrs Twiddle. 'And you kept on picking it up and losing it and picking it up – oh, Twiddle, I think my cat's got more sense in its head than you have. Wasting all the morning doing a silly thing like that!'

Twiddle was very upset. He picked up a twenty pence by his foot and absent-mindedly put it into his pocket. It at once fell out and appeared by his foot again.

'See! That's what's been happening all the time,' said Mrs Twiddle. 'Now, you listen to me, Twiddle – I shan't give you any dinner at all till you've finished cutting this grass. So, if you want to play with the cat or go on picking up your money, you know what to expect!'

And little Mrs Twiddle walked back to the house quite crossly. Twiddle sighed loudly, took his scythe and set to work.

What a disappointment – and how cross Mrs Twiddle looked. Then a thought came into Twiddle's head. He threw down his scythe and ran across the garden till he came to the kitchen window. He popped his head in and made Mrs Twiddle jump.

'Now, you listen to me,' said Twiddle, quite

fiercely. 'Do you know whose fault all this is? Yours, yours! And do you know why? Because you didn't mend the hole in my pocket! Aha! Aha!'

Then, feeling quite pleased with himself, Twiddle went happily back to the grass and scythed hard till it was all cut. And you will be glad to know that Mrs Twiddle had a lovely dinner ready for him, and gave him a hearty kiss when he came in.

'You're a dear old thing, even if you *are* stupid!' she said. 'Now, don't you dare to say Aha! to me again, or I shall laugh till I cry. Aha, indeed!'

Chapter 4

A Knot in Twiddle's Hanky

'I do wish I could remember things,' said Mr Twiddle in despair. 'I meant to go and fetch my shoes before the shops closed, so that I could go for a nice walk this evening – and I forgot.'

'And you can't possibly go for a walk in those old shoes you're wearing,' said Mrs Twiddle. 'Why don't you tie a knot in your hanky, or something, Twiddle, then you would see it and remember you had to do something?'

'Well, that's just what I *will* do!' said Mr Twiddle, and he took out his big red handkerchief and tied a large knot at one corner. 'There! Now, when I see that knot I shall know I must remember something.'

'What are you going to remember?' asked Mrs Twiddle, with a little squeal of laughter.

'Oh, dear me, yes – I forgot I had to have something to remember, before I tied a knot,' said Mr Twiddle. 'Well, I know – I really must remember to fetch my shoes tomorrow. I'll leave the knot in for that.'

So he left it in, and went to read his paper in the garden. Before very long he took out his red hanky to mop his head – and he saw the knot.

'Aha! The knot! Now that was to make sure I remembered something. What was it?'

But for the life of him poor Mr Twiddle couldn't remember what the knot was for! So he called his wife. 'Can you think of anything I said I would do, and haven't done?' he asked.

'Good gracious, yes!' said Mrs Twiddle at once, thinking of a whole lot of things. 'What about cutting the grass?'

'Oh, dear – did I really put the knot in my hanky for that?' said Mr Twiddle, with a sigh. 'Well, well – it's no good putting knots in if I don't take any notice of them.' So he got up, fetched the lawn-mower and began to cut the grass.

He was so hot when he had finished that he sat down on the seat to rest. He pulled out his hanky – and in it he saw the knot again. He had forgotten to undo it! So he thought it was another knot, of course. He stared at it, frowning.

'Good gracious! Now what's *this* knot for? he wondered. He called to his wife. 'Is there anything else I ought to do?'

'Dear me, yes! What about weeding the lettuces?' called back his wife, giggling to herself to think that dear old Twiddle hadn't undone the knot.

Twiddle got up. 'Well, I never! Was that what the knot was for in my hanky? What a memory I've got, to be sure.'

So off he went to weed the lettuce bed, and it took him till supper-time. He was really very tired when he went in.

After his supper he took out his hanky to wipe some crumbs off his waistcoat – and again he saw the very same knot.

'Look at that!' he said to his wife, who turned away to laugh all by herself. 'What's *that* knot for, I'd like to know?'

'You haven't filled the coal bucket for me,' said Mrs Twiddle. 'Would it be that, Twiddle?'

'It might be,' said Twiddle. 'Anyway, I'll do it. Oh, dear, what a pity I saw the knot!'

He saw it again just before he went to bed. 'Bless us all! Here's a knot in my hanky again!' he said to his wife. 'The things I have to remember! What can it be now? Is there anything important I must do?'

'Yes. Put the cat out, and then get her in again,' said Mrs Twiddle, getting ready to go up to bed. 'You always forget that, Twiddle.'

Twiddle groaned. 'That cat! I let her in and out all day long. She just does it on purpose. And yet at night, when I kindly open the door for her without her asking me, she won't go out. Puss, come along! Out you go!'

Mrs Twiddle had gone upstairs by the time Mr Twiddle had let the cat out and waited patiently for it to come back again. He went up and got into bed beside his plump little wife.

He took his hanky to put under the pillow – and dear me, he saw the knot again! Yes, the very same knot.

Mrs Twiddle was asleep. Twiddle couldn't bear to wake her. He stared at the knot and tried to puzzle out what it was there to remind him of. To fasten all the windows? To rake out the kitchen fire? To see if the larder door was safely shut? To – to – to – well, what *was* it for?

Poor Twiddle got out of bed, put on his dressing-gown and went downstairs to see if he could find something he had forgotten to do. But he couldn't. The doors were locked, the windows were fastened, the larder was shut, the fire was raked out. Then what could it be?

He went into the sitting-room to see if everything was all right there, and fell over the cat, which got between his legs in her usual annoying way. He fell down with a crash, knocked over a little table, and down went Mrs Twiddle's best fern!

Mrs Twiddle woke up with a dreadful jump. 'Twiddle!' she said sharply. 'Burglars! Quick, Twiddle!'

But Twiddle wasn't there. Mrs Twiddle put on her dressing-gown and went downstairs in time to see Twiddle pelting the cat with the earth out of her plant pot! She was very cross indeed.

'Really, Twiddle! Have you *got* to do this sort of thing in the middle of the night when

I'm sound asleep? The poor cat! And my poor fern! Puss, Puss, come to me, then. Naughty Twiddle, what was he doing to you?'

'*Well*!' said Twiddle, annoyed. 'I like *that*! Why don't you ask your cat what she was doing to me? Tripping me up on purpose!'

'What did you come down for?' asked Mrs Twiddle, crossly.

'Well – to see if I'd forgotten to do something,' said Twiddle. 'But everything seems all right. I'm coming to bed. But that cat isn't. Leave her in the kitchen, please.'

Poor Pussy!' said Mrs Twiddle, and put the cat down. They went up to bed together and took off their dressing-gowns. Just as he got into bed Twiddle saw his hanky on the pillow and stared at the knot.

'That knot again!' he cried. 'What's it to remind me of *now*, I'd like to know. I'll never put another knot in my hanky again!'

'You won't need to!' said Mrs Twiddle, with a laugh. 'You seem to keep the same one in all the time. You never undo it! Oh, Twiddle, you'll be the death of me one day, with your foolish ways. Now, you listen to me – that knot is to tell you to lie down, shut your eyes and go to sleep!'

'Is it really?' said Twiddle, blowing out his candle and lying down very thankfully. 'Well, well – to think I put a knot in my hanky to remind me to do something I could *never* forget to do!'

And off he went to sleep. But I wonder if he'll remember to fetch his shoes next day? Do you think he will?

Chapter 5

Mr Twiddle Goes Shopping

'Twiddle, you are not listening to anything I'm saying!' said Mrs Twiddle, crossly. 'There you sit in your chair, reading your newspaper and not paying any attention to me at all.'

'But you were only talking abut your shopping, my love,' said Mr Twiddle.

'I know – but *you* are to do the shopping for me today, so I want you to listen!' scolded Mrs Twiddle.

'Aren't you going to make me out a list?' said Mr Twiddle. 'You always take a list yourself.'

'Yes, of course I shall make you a list – but you must listen to me all the same,' said Mrs Twiddle.

'Very well, my dear,' said Mr Twiddle, but he didn't listen. He went on reading his paper, and all that Mrs Twiddle said went in at one ear and out at the other.

Somebody came to the door and Mrs Twiddle went to open it. When she came back, she had Twiddle's hat and coat and scarf in her hands.

'Here you are, Twiddle,' she said. 'Put these on and go quickly, or everything in the shops will be sold. Hurry!'

'You always want things done in such a

hurry,' grumbled Twiddle, putting down his paper and getting up.

He put on his coat and hat and Mrs Twiddle tied his scarf round his neck. Then she gave him a kiss. 'There you are, grumbler. And here is your shopping list. Take the basket and be sure to bring me back everything on the list.

Twiddle put the list in his pocket, picked up the basket, fell over the cat, and went out. It was a nice, bright, frosty day. Twiddle walked fast because it was cold.

He looked at his list. 'Butter, Soles, Drops, Corn, Hooks, Cake,' he read. 'Well, butter is easy. I'll call at the grocer's for that straight away.'

He collected the butter. 'Soles,' he thought. 'Good gracious! Does Mrs Twiddle want soles for her shoes – or soles to eat? Goodness knows!'

He thought the best thing to do would be to buy a pair of soles at the fish shop, and a pair of soles at the shoe shop. Then whatever happened, he would be right. So that is what he did! Into his basket went the fish, also the soles to go inside slippers.

He looked at the list again. 'Drops!

Goodness gracious, what kind of drops? Snowdrops? Peppermint drops? Eye drops? Which did Mrs Twiddle say?'

Well, of course, as Twiddle hadn't listened at all to what Mrs Twiddle said to him he had no idea which to buy. He decided to get some more eye drops at the chemist's. Mrs Twiddle had weak eyes and she sometimes put drops into them at night. She might have meant those.

On the other hand she might have meant peppermint drops, which she liked very much. Very well, Mr Twiddle would get those too! So he went to the sweet shop and bought fifty pence-worth of peppermint drops.

Then he suddenly saw a woman selling bunches of snowdrops at the kerb. Snow*drops*! Well, well – Mrs Twiddle *might* have meant those. So he bought a little bunch and put it into his basket.

What was next on the list? Corn? Ah, corn, that was easy. But wait a minute – did Mrs Twiddle want corn for her hens, or a corn-cure for that big corn she was always complaining about? Twiddle decided to buy both, then Mrs Twiddle couldn't possibly grumble at him.

So he bought a bag of corn, which was very heavy, and a bottle of corn-cure. What next?

'Hooks. Hooks! Gracious, what kind of hooks? Hooks and eyes – curtain hooks – or crochet hooks?' wondered poor Mr Twiddle. 'Can't be curtain hooks, because she isn't hanging up any curtains. It must be crochet hooks – or hooks and eyes. I'll buy both and after that I'll buy the cake.'

It was a very, very heavy basket that Mr Twiddle took home. He decided to ask Mrs Twiddle to read down the list to him, and then he would hand out the things she said – perhaps she would add a little explanation as she read them. She might say 'soles for our supper,' then he would know that meant the fish, and not the slipper soles, and he would hand out the right thing.

'Hello, Twiddle dear, what a long time you've been!' said Mrs Twiddle, when he went into the house. 'Have you got every thing? I do hope you have. They were all most important.'

Mr Twiddle hoped he had got them too. Mrs Twiddle wouldn't be at all pleased if he had bought the wrong things!

'Read down the list, dear, and I'll hand out

the things,' said Twiddle. Mrs Twiddle took the list and began to read. 'Butter, Twiddle – did you get it?'

'Here it is,' said Twiddle, and handed it out. 'Next, please?'

'Soles, Twiddle. I do hope the fishmonger hadn't sold out,' said Mrs Twiddle. That was a most helpful remark. Mr Twiddle at once handed out the fish.

'The drops,' said Mrs Twiddle. 'Had the chemist got them?'

'Ah,' thought Twiddle, as he handed out the eye drops, 'this is fine! What a good idea of mine to get Mrs Twiddle to read out the list!'

'Corn,' said Mrs Twiddle. 'Ah, there it is in that bag. What a lovely lot you've brought, Twiddle! The hens *will* enjoy themselves!'

'Easier and easier!' thought Twiddle, feeling very pleased. 'What's next?'

'Hooks,' said Mrs Twiddle. 'Did you get them?'

Ah – now Twiddle didn't know which hooks to hand out – the hooks and eyes – or the crochet hooks! He pretended to stop and think whether he had got them or not.

'Oh, don't say you forgot my hooks and

eyes!' said Mrs Twiddle. 'I *told* you I wanted to sew them on to my new dress tonight. Oh, Twiddle!'

'Yes, yes, I got them!' said Twiddle delighted, and handed out the little packet. 'And here's the cake. That was the last thing on the list, wasn't it?'

'How clever you are!' said Mrs Twiddle. She looked at the basket. 'Why, you've got lots more things there, Twiddle? Snowdrops! How lovely! Are they for me?

'Yes,' said Twiddle, beaming. 'Of course.'

'Oh, how kind you are. And what are

these?' said Mrs Twiddle, opening the bag. 'Peppermint drops! How did you guess I had none left? And, oh, Twiddle, you don't mean to tell me you remembered to buy a pair of soles to put in my old bedroom slippers! How wonderful!'

'Well,' began Twiddle, 'you see –'

But Mrs Twiddle cut him short and gave him a hug. 'Thank you, thank you,' she said. 'They're lovely and just the right size.'

She dived into the basket again. 'Oh, Twiddle, you've bought me a new corn-cure for my poor corn – and you've got some new crochet hooks for me, too. You are really very kind and generous!'

Twiddle felt so pleased. He had done better than he thought! Mrs Twiddle flew round him; and found his slippers and his pipe. She gave him his newspaper, and made up the fire.

'Now you sit down and have a good read!' she said. 'And I'll make you toast and dripping for your tea. You deserve a treat, you nice, kind man!'

Well, he did really, didn't he – and how he enjoyed it!

Chapter 6

Mr Twiddle's Shadow

Mr Twiddle was very angry with the cat. He spoke to it very sternly indeed.

'Now you listen to me, Cat! You have a good home here and plenty to eat, and a nice basket of your own. And what do you do? You steal things out of the larder if the door is left open so much as a crack, and you . . .'

The cat turned its back on Mr Twiddle and began to wash itself, wetting its paws and rubbing them over its face.

'Turn round!' said Mr Twiddle, in a rage. 'Don't you know your manners? I'm talking to you. Stop doing that soap-and-flannel act of yours, washing your silly face over and over, and look at me!'

The cat didn't. It just went on washing

itself. Twiddle marched round to the other side of it and addressed it again.

'All right!' If you think you can turn your back on me, you're wrong. Now, just let me tell you the things you've done to annoy me today. I left the breakfast table for just one moment and what did you do? Jumped up and ate all my bacon. And you . . .'

The cat turned its back to Twiddle again and began to wash another bit of itself. Twiddle flew into a real temper and stamped his foot. He began to shout.

'Rude creature! You stole my bacon, you made me open the window twice – once for you to come in and once for you to go out – and you tripped me up in the passage when I was carrying the milk. You did it on purpose so that you could lick up the milk!'

The cat walked haughtily to the door, stood by it, miaowed, and looked round at Twiddle.

'Ha! Now you're ordering me to open the door, are you?' said Twiddle. 'Well, I won't. I've had enough of you, see? I shall not open another window or door for you all my life long!'

The cat sat down patiently by the door and began to wash itself again. Twiddle went on muttering. The kettle began to boil on the stove. Twiddle ran to take it off before it dripped all over the place.

The cat ran, too, and tripped up Twiddle as neatly as could be.

Down he went with the kettle and a tiny drop of the scalding water went over the cat. She set up such a hullabaloo that Mrs Twiddle came rushing into the kitchen.

She was just in time to see Twiddle give the cat a most resounding whack. She was horrified.

'TWIDDLE! What are you doing to MY cat?

I saw you smack it – and oh, poor thing, it must have got its tail scalded by the hot water!'

'It's been licking itself all morning,' said Twiddle. 'What about *me*? I've scalded myself, too – look, on my hand. That cat tripped me up on purpose to make me spill the water. Yes, I smacked it – and if it sits and looks at me like that I'll smack it again!'

'TWIDDLE!' cried Mrs Twiddle, amazed. 'This isn't like you. You sound so hard and cruel.'

'I *feel* hard and cruel,' said poor Twiddle, holding his scalded hand. 'I hope I've done the cat a lot of good, giving her a good smack like that. For two pins I'd give her another.'

'Now, stop, Twiddle,' said his wife, getting very stern. 'It doesn't do her any good to smack her.'

'How do you know?' said Twiddle. 'You've never smacked her. I tell you smacking is what she wants. I tell you smacking will make a different cat of her.'

'Well, it won't,' said Mrs Twiddle. 'It will just make her hate and hate you, Twiddle. You're very unkind indeed. That poor cat will never go near you again.'

'Well, that will be a very good thing,' said Twiddle. 'All the same I still say that smack has done her good.'

Mrs Twiddle was cross with him. She put on what Twiddle called her 'haughty face' and he didn't like it a bit. 'She keeps looking at me as if I was something on the rubbish heap,' he grumbled to himself. 'Oh dear, how long is she going to keep this up? It will make me miserable.'

The cat didn't go near Twiddle. It kept round Mrs Twiddle and mewed pitifully. Twiddle knew it was just making a fuss. Mrs Twiddle gave it all kinds of titbits and petted it and fussed it till poor Twiddle nearly went mad. Had that smack done it any good after all? If only it had!

Mrs Twiddle was so cold to poor Twiddle all day long that he really couldn't bear it. He very nearly said he was sorry he had been unkind to the cat, and only just stopped himself in time.

Then an idea came to him. It was a very silly idea, but still it *was* an idea. Mr Twiddle put on his coat and hat and called to his wife.

'Just going to get an evening paper!'

And off he went. He bought the paper and

then he went to the fishmonger's, where he bought a pound of yesterday's fish. It wasn't very fresh and the fishmonger was rather surprised at Twiddle picking out stale fish. Still, he didn't mind selling it, so off went Twiddle, the fish under his arm.

When he got to the field not far from his home, Mr Twiddle began to act in a most peculiar manner. He stepped into the field, looked cautiously round to make sure no one was watching him, and undid the parcel of stale fish. He spread it on the grass and then stamped on it! How he stamped! He jumped up and down on it too, and he even wiped the fish paper round his boots.

'There!' said Twiddle, walking out of the field and leaving the stale, jumped-on fish behind. 'Now if that cat doesn't follow me round like a shadow all this evening I shall be very surprised! Ha! Mrs Twiddle said the cat would never come near me again – but she will!'

He went in at the back door. Mrs Twiddle was in the kitchen, sweeping up some crumbs. The cat was sitting haughtily in the scullery. It gave Twiddle a very nasty look.

Twiddle walked in boldly, and pretended to aim a kick at the cat. It caught a whiff of the fishy smell on his boots, and opened its eyes wide. It sat up straight. My, what a wonderful smell!

Twiddle walked through into the kitchen. The cat followed at once, sniffing eagerly. It came right to Twiddle's heels. Mrs Twiddle looked up, still with her 'haughty face'. She was surprised to see the cat following Twiddle so closely.

'Nice and cosy in here,' said Twiddle, amiably. 'I'll just hang my things in the hall.'

He went into the hall. The cat followed closely at his heels and came back at his heels, too, feeling excited. Twiddle had never smelt so nice before. Where *had* he been, thought the cat.

Twiddle walked through the kitchen and into the scullery, just to let his wife see the cat following him again. Mrs Twiddle said nothing, but she couldn't help feeling more and more astonished. She knew her cat. It was a touchy cat. Even a cross word made it sulk, and it never had liked Mr Twiddle, who was very free with his cross words at times.

'I'm just going to get the wood in for the morning,' said Twiddle, and he walked out into the garden. The cat followed him, almost bumping its nose into his heels.

'Call your cat,' said Twiddle, stopping so suddenly that the cat *did* bump its nose. 'It's better in the warm kitchen.'

'Puss, Puss!' called Mrs Twiddle. 'Come to me, Puss dear!'

Puss-dear took not the slightest notice. She began to purr round Twiddle, and even rubbed her head against his legs. Mrs Twiddle simply couldn't understand it.

'PUSS!' she called sharply. She didn't like

the cat not coming to her when it was called. The cat gave her a sour look, and went on purring round Twiddle.

'Oh well, if she wants to be my shadow, let her!' said Twiddle airily, and went to the wood-shed, followed by the cat.

He came back with the cat. He went upstairs and the cat went too. He went to wash his hands in the bathroom and when Mrs Twiddle popped her head round the door, there was the cat, almost sitting on Twiddle's feet.

Twiddle came into the kitchen with the purring cat. He sat down in his chair. 'Now,' he said sternly to the cat, 'I do *not* want you on my knee. I am still not pleased with you. Just remember that hard smack I gave you this morning, and behave yourself!'

The cat didn't attempt to jump up as she usually did. She sat down contentedly at Twiddle's feet, so that the fishy smell on his boots kept coming to her nose. She suddenly turned her head and began to lick his boots with her pink tongue.

Mrs Twiddle was ironing and watching all the time. She put down her iron. 'Twiddle,' she said, in a much nicer voice than she had spoken to him all day, 'Twiddle, look at that cat – it's licking your boots!'

'Yes, I know. It's learnt that I'm master at last,' said Twiddle comfortably. 'I told you that a smack would do it good. It knows it's got to mind its *p's and q's* with me now. Any more nonsense from it and it will get another smack.'

Mrs Twiddle didn't say a word to that. She was thinking very hard. She had never seen the cat so attached to Twiddle before. Why, Twiddle might be its best friend instead of someone who had scalded it and smacked it not very many hours ago! Could it be that Twiddle was right? Did it need a good smack sometimes?

She went on ironing. The cat licked Twiddle's boots a bit longer, then lay down on his feet and went to sleep.

Mrs Twiddle simply could not get over its behaviour.

'Twiddle,' she said, after a bit, 'there's a funny sort of smell in this kitchen, isn't there? A sort of fishy smell.'

'Nonsense, my dear!' said Twiddle at once. 'Drains, I expect. You're always imagining things.'

'I hope the cat hasn't had the fish out of the larder,' said Mrs Twiddle, and she went to look. 'If she has I shall give her a good smack!'

That was too much for Mr Twiddle. He burst into such a loud laugh that the cat nearly jumped out of its skin. 'That's right,' said Twiddle. 'I tell you, this cat is all the better for a good smack!'

He went out to post a letter, later on, not because he wanted to, but because he meant to show Mrs Twiddle that the cat would even go out to walk with him. It did, of course, keeping to his heels like a shadow again. Mrs Twiddle was most impressed.

Twiddle sat down again when he got in. 'Here are your slippers, Twiddle, dear,' said Mrs Twiddle, in a meek voice, when he came in. 'I've warmed them for you.'

Twiddle was about to take them when he remembered not to. It would never do to take off his fishy boots – the cat would desert him at once! 'Can't be bothered to put on my slippers,' he said, much to Mrs Twiddle's astonishment. Really, what with Twiddle's behaviour and the cat's, she felt quite bewildered!

'Now, listen. I won't have the cat wandering up into our bedroom tonight,' said Twiddle, sternly, when he and his wife were ready to go to bed. 'I'm tired of her sleeping on my middle. I can't think why she never sleeps on yours. She must stay down here in the scullery.'

'She won't,' said Mrs Twiddle.

'She will,' said Twiddle. He took off his

boots and took them into the scullery. He stood them by the door to clean them in the morning. Then he spoke sternly to the cat.

'Cat! Sit down there by my boots and don't stir from them all night long. Do you hear?'

'Miaow,' said the cat, obediently, and lay down as close to the fishy boots as she possibly could. Mrs Twiddle could hardly believe her eyes.

'I think you're rather a wonderful man, Twiddle,' she said, when they went upstairs. 'Honestly, I never saw the cat so well behaved – why, it was just like your shadow.'

'Well, just you be firm with it,' said Twiddle. 'And mind you back me up when it annoys me. Next time it trips me up and I smack it, you must smack it, too.'

'Oh, I think one smack would be enough,' said kind Mrs Twiddle. 'Well, well, to think of that cat adoring you all evening like that! Who would have thought it? I feel quite jealous!'

'Oh, it will stop bothering itself about me tomorrow,' said Mr Twiddle, getting into bed, 'and it will follow you around just as usual. You'll see!'

It will, of course, because old Twiddle will

have cleaned his boots and they won't smell fishy any more!

The thing is, he sometimes forgets to clean them, and if Mrs Twiddle happens to do them for him, *what* will she think of the fishy smell? Twiddle, be sure you don't forget!

Chapter 7

When Mr Twiddle Was Asleep

'I don't know when I've felt so sleepy,' said Mr Twiddle, yawning, one afternoon.

'You always do feel sleepy in the afternoon,' said Mrs Twiddle, bustling round. 'And you always say exactly what you've just said. Now, Twiddle, I'm going out to see old Mrs Tabbit. You stay here in case anyone comes to the door.'

'Right!' said Twiddle, pleased at the idea of a peaceful afternoon in front of the fire. 'Is anyone likely to come?'

'No,' said Mrs Twiddle. 'And, Twiddle, see that the door is kept shut, will you, so that the cat doesn't get in and wander round. She'll try to get my knitting if she can. She's been a naughty puss lately over that.'

73

'I'll be very pleased to keep the cat out,' said Twiddle, settling down in his chair and opening his newspaper. 'Nothing I should like better. The longer she's out the more I'll be pleased.'

Mrs Twiddle put on her hat and coat and said goodbye. 'Now have a good snooze, she said. 'You really do look rather tired – been reading the newspaper too much, I expect! Goodbye, Twiddle dear.'

'Goodbye, my love,' said Twiddle, feeling very amiable indeed. Fancy having an afternoon with nobody telling him to do this, that and the other – and the cat forbidden to come in, too! Now she wouldn't be able to sit herself on his knee all the afternoon and dig her claws into him. Aha! this was wonderful.

He was asleep before Mrs Twiddle had passed by the window. She had a look in and smiled to herself. 'Poor old Twiddle – he really *is* tired today!' she thought. 'I do hope nothing disturbs him.'

She went on her way to Mrs Tabbit's. Halfway there she met Mr Screw, the carpenter. He nodded to her.

'You naughty man!' said Mrs Twiddle, playfully. 'You haven't been to do the lock of my kitchen door yet – and it *is* so difficult to lock.'

'Well, there, ma'am – if I hadn't forgotten all about it!' said Mr Screw. He was a great big man, with a shock of red hair and a big nose. 'I'm down right sorry. Look, I've got a bit of time this afternoon. I'll go right along and do it now.'

'Oh, that *would* be nice of you,' said Mrs Twiddle. 'Could you really? The only thing is – you'll disturb Mr Twiddle. He's asleep in the kitchen and really very tired.'

'He sleeps so soundly that he won't hear.

me,' said Mr Screw. 'I'll be very quiet, ma'am. He won't know I've been.'

So off he hurried to Twiddle's house. He was soon there. He peeped in at the kitchen window and saw Twiddle fast asleep. He went to the door and opened it.

He examined the lock. Dear, dear, he hadn't got the right tools with him – and if he tried to do it without them he would probably make a tremendous noise, and that would wake up Mr Twiddle.

Mr Screw scratched his head. If he went to fetch the right tools, and came back again, he'd be late for his next job. What could he do? Perhaps he had better make a noise after all and chance waking up Mr Twiddle?

'No, I won't do that,' said the carpenter suddenly. 'I know a better idea. I'll simply take the door off its hinges and carry it home with me – do the lock there and carry the door back. It won't take me any time then.'

So, very quietly, he began to take the door off its hinges. The cat came and watched him with much interest. She hadn't seen a door taken off before. She was pleased. Now she could get into the warm kitchen and perhaps find something to eat.

'Miaow!' said the cat and rubbed herself against the carpenter.

'Sh!' said the carpenter. 'You'll wake Mr Twiddle.'

The cat didn't mind about that at all, and went on miaowing. But Twiddle didn't stir. He was fast asleep and dreaming a wonderful dream about a dish of fried steak and onions that never grew smaller however much he ate of it. He snored a little.

Soon the carpenter had the door right off. He lifted it up on his shoulder and went off with it. The cat shot into the room as soon as the doorway was empty and leapt on to Twiddle's knee, digging her claws into him as usual.

Twiddle woke up with a jump. He stared at the cat in anger. 'How did *you* get in?' he asked, exasperated. 'Door and window shut and yet you appear. Get down from my knee at once.'

'Miaow,' said the cat, and tried to rub her head against Twiddle's chin. That was too much. He put her down and shut his eyes again. 'I don't know how you got in, but you can go out the same way,' he said.

An icy draught blew round his chair.

Twiddle sat up and looked at the fire. Had it gone down while he was asleep? Why was the room so cold?

No, the fire was beautiful. He sat back again and shut his eyes. But a little wind lifted his hair at the top, where it showed above the chair. Twiddle was puzzled. *Where* was this frightful draught coming from?

He looked round his chair – and to his enormous surprise, he saw the empty doorway. The wind was blowing through and making the place as cold as could be.

Twiddle didn't notice that the door was gone at first – he simply thought it was wide open. He glared at the cat. 'Did *you* manage to open that door on your own, you maddening, tiresome cat?'

The cat said nothing but began to wash herself. Twiddle got up and went to shut the door.

But the door, of course, wasn't there. Twiddle stared as if he couldn't believe his eyes. He ran his hand round the doorway – no, there was no door at all. It had absolutely vanished!

'Well – I must still be asleep, that's all,' said Twiddle, bewildered. 'I'll go and sit down again and maybe the door will be back again when I next wake up.'

So he went and sat down again – but he was so puzzled that he couldn't go to sleep. He kept looking round his chair at the empty doorway, and shivering in the draught.

'Somebody must have stolen the door!' he said to himself at last. 'A thief must have crept up when I was asleep, and taken the door off – the wicked robber!'

He went into the garden and called his

next-door neighbour. 'Hey! Did you see a man carrying a door this afternoon?'

The neighbour stared. 'No. Why should I? People don't usually go about carrying doors.'

'Well, *someone* is going about carrying a door,' said Twiddle, suddenly feeling very fierce indeed, 'and what's more I'm going to find out who it is!'

He rushed indoors, fell over the cat, got his hat and stick and rushed out. He trotted into the town, looking everywhere for a man carrying a door. But there wasn't one to be seen anywhere. This wasn't surprising, because the carpenter was now busily mending the lock in his own workroom.

As soon as he had finished it, he popped the door on his shoulder again and off he went back to Mr Twiddle's house. By that time Twiddle was at the other end of the town, walking up the steps to the police station, looking very fierce indeed.

'What do you want, sir?' asked the constable there.

'Someone's stolen my door!' said Twiddle, and he banged his hand on the desk. 'I want it back!'

'What door?' asked the policeman, astonished.

'My kitchen door,' said Mr Twiddle. 'When I was fast asleep, too. Taken it right away.'

'Er – well – this is very peculiar,' said the constable, and reached for his helmet. 'I'll come with you and make a report, sir.'

Twiddle marched him all the way to his house. He went down the back path to the kitchen door. 'This is where the door was stolen,' he said, and stopped suddenly.

The door was back! There it was, fast shut, and looking very solid indeed. Mr Screw had put it back five minutes before and had then gone off again.

The policeman stared stolidly at the door. 'Are you playing a joke on me?' he enquired.

Mr Twiddle looked scared. He felt the door gingerly. It was real and solid – but when he had left the house it hadn't been there. Now it was back! He simply couldn't understand it!

'Er – very peculiar,' said Mr Twiddle, still staring at the door. 'It wasn't there when I left. Now it's come back.'

'Doors don't come and go like that,' said the constable, putting away his notebook. 'I don't suppose you took a good look, sir – the

81

door must have been there all the time. Good afternoon.'

Mrs Twiddle came in at that moment and was most surprised to see a policeman going out of the back gate. She hurried up to Twiddle, who was still standing outside the back door, looking puzzled.

'Twiddle, what have you been up to? Why did that policeman call?' she panted.

'Well – er – it was nothing much,' said . Twiddle, suddenly feeling that he didn't really want to discuss vanishing doors with Mrs Twiddle. He didn't feel that she would believe him. 'He – er – well, he just came about a door.'

'About a *door*.' said Mrs Twiddle, even more astonished. 'What door?'

She opened the kitchen door and went inside. The very first thing she saw was the cat playing with her knitting! It had rolled the ball of wool all over the place, and had undone half the jumper she was making. Now it was busy chewing her needles!

She gave a scream. 'Oh, you wicked cat! Get her out, quick, Twiddle!'

Twiddle was only too pleased. He grabbed at the cat, which dodged aside, and Twiddle hit his hand hard against the dresser. The cat fled out of the open door.

'You deserve to go out, too, Twiddle,' said Mrs Twiddle angrily. 'Didn't I *ask* you not to let the cat in?'

'I didn't let her in,' said Twiddle, sucking his hand.

'Well, you must have done. She can't come in through a shut door,' said Mrs Twiddle.

'She did,' said Twiddle. 'But wait a minute – perhaps she didn't. Perhaps she came in after the door was gone!'

'Gone?' said Mrs Twiddle, staring at Twiddle. '*Gone*? What do you mean – *gone*? Doors don't go.'

'This one did,' said Twiddle; 'I fetched the police about it. And when we came back, the door had come again.'

'Twiddle, dear, do you feel quite well?' said Mrs Twiddle, suddenly, thinking he must be going mad or something. 'Would you like to go to bed?'

Twiddle thought it would be a good idea. Then perhaps he wouldn't have to do any more explaining about cats and knitting and doors that came and went.

'I think I *will* go to bed,' said Twiddle. So up he went. Mrs Twiddle fussed over him like anything. She gave him a hot-water bottle, she brought him hot milk, she even went out to buy him a late newspaper. He was tremendously pleased. He really enjoyed himself.

He's never found out why the door came and went, because the carpenter didn't bother to tell Mrs Twiddle about it. Mr Twiddle would have forgotten all about it long ago, if it wasn't that he keeps meeting the policeman he fetched that day.

'Morning, Mr Twiddle,' the policeman says each time. 'Had any more trouble with your *doors*?'

Dear old Twiddle! I can't help liking him, can you?

Chapter 8

Twiddle Goes for a Walk

Mrs Twiddle bustled in just at teatime. It was a winter's evening, and already almost dark outside. She called Twiddle.

'Twiddle! Twiddle! Where are you? Have you got the tea ready as I told you?'

Twiddle hadn't. He had gone to sleep in front of the kitchen fire, and had only just woken up when he heard Mrs Twiddle come in. He was now scurrying round filling the kettle, putting it on the stove, and trying to get out all the tea things at once!

'Twiddle! Can't you hear me? I'm home!' called Mrs Twiddle, walking into the kitchen. 'Dear me – you haven't even got the tea laid.'

'Just ready, *just* ready!' said Twiddle,

banging the loaf down on the platter. 'You must be early, my dear.'

'No, I'm not!' said Mrs Twiddle, taking off her hat. 'I'm late. And I'm tired and thirsty. I suppose you slept in front of the kitchen fire from the moment I went out and shut the door to the moment I came back, Twiddle. And I suppose you haven't done a single thing I asked you to – not one!'

Twiddle fell over the cat and didn't answer. He glared at the cat. 'Did you do that on purpose, you miserable animal? How did you get in? You were outside when I began to get tea.'

'Oh, Twiddle – she must have got in through the bedroom window,' said Mrs Twiddle. 'And I *asked* you to be sure and shut it if it rained. You can't have shut it. Did you?'

As Twiddle hadn't even known it had been raining that afternoon he certainly hadn't shut the window. Trust that cat to give him away!

'And did you fetch in some more coal as I asked you?' asked Mrs Twiddle. 'Oh, dear – no, you didn't! The scuttle is empty. And did you take the clothes in off the line? Oh, Twiddle – they're still there. I can see them

flapping in the darkness. They'll be soaked
with the rain! And what about the dog? Did
you take him for a short walk?'

Twiddle hadn't done anything at all except
go to sleep. He felt very much ashamed of
himself. Dear, dear – he hadn't even *thought*
about the dog!

'Oh, Twiddle – I do think you are very, very
mean,' said poor Mrs Twiddle, sitting down.
'I've been busy all the afternoon nursing my
poor sister, and I did so want my tea ready
when I got home. I don't believe you love me
one bit. Not one bit. You haven't done a thing
I asked you.'

To Twiddle's horror she burst into tears. He hurried over with his big hanky, but she pushed him away.

'No! You don't love me!' she sobbed. 'I know you don't. You just went to sleep and forgot all about me.'

Twiddle felt very guilty indeed. He felt lazy and unkind and selfish and good-for-nothing. He tried again to dry his wife's eyes. But she wouldn't let him. Twiddle was very miserable.

What could he do to put things right? He rushed about, made the tea, cut bread and butter and put out cakes. He tore out into the darkness and brought in the clothes from the line. He fell over the cat again, and didn't say a word. He rushed upstairs and shut the bedroom window, because it was raining once more. He went out and got some more coal in. The cat went with him, very interested in Twiddle's sudden fit of hurry-scurry.

He nearly fell over her again. He didn't say a word but pushed her into the coal cellar and shut the door firmly. 'You'll be out of my way in there,' he whispered, when he had banged the door. The cat settled down on the coal and began to wash herself. She quite liked the coal cellar.

But still Mrs Twiddle wouldn't forgive poor Twiddle. She ate her tea in silence. She wouldn't look at him. It was really dreadful.

Twiddle couldn't eat anything, he was so upset. What else could he do to show his wife that he was very sorry? He sat and thought. Then he got up and took down his hat and coat. 'I'm going to take the poor dog for a run,' he said. 'I'll fetch him from his kennel.'

The rain was pelting against the windows, and Twiddle did hope that Mrs Twiddle would say no, he wasn't to go out in such a downpour. But she didn't. She just sat and drank her tea and wouldn't even *look* at poor Twiddle! So out he went into the rain and darkness, and made his way to the kennel.

Rain or not, the dog was very glad to see him. He would hardly stand still for Twiddle to put on his lead. In the end Twiddle dropped it on the ground and couldn't find it again in the darkness. Oh, dear! He really didn't want to go back into the house to get a torch to look for the lead. So he took a bit of rope and tied that through the dog's collar instead.

He set off with the dog in the rain. He hadn't got an umbrella, so he soon got wet.

He was hungry and thirsty because he hadn't had any tea. He was also very miserable. So was the dog, because he didn't think walks in the rain and darkness were much fun – and he didn't like a silent, unhappy master.

Twiddle soon came to the town. He came to a brightly lit little place called 'Tilly's Tea Room.' A nice smell of toast came out from the door. It made Mr Twiddle feel very hungry indeed. He knew this tea room. It was a place where farmers came after market to have tea and toast and new-baked ginger cake. Outside was a strong railing to which they could tie their horses, cows, a sheep or two, and dogs.

Twiddle decided to go in and have some tea and toast. He tied the dog firmly to the railings by his rope. 'Shan't be long, old fellow,' he said. 'It's stopped raining now so you'll be all right.'

Twiddle enjoyed his tea and toast and new ginger cake. Then he thought he had better be getting back because Mrs Twiddle might think he was out too long. So he paid his bill and got up to go.

It was pitch dark outside now. Twiddle wished and wished he had brought a torch.

He groped his way to the railing and fell over what seemed to be a pig, by its excited grunts. He felt about for his dog.

'Where are you?' he said, and the dog barked gladly. Twiddle undid the rope from the railing and set off home.

'Come along,' he said. 'We'll get back. I shall be glad of my warm fire and you'll be glad of your cosy kennel.'

He walked home quickly, glad that it had stopped raining. He took the dog to its kennel and shut it in, giving it a push because it didn't seem to want to go in. Then he went indoors, hoping that Mrs Twiddle was in a better temper now.

But she wasn't. 'Where's the cat?' she asked him. 'I can hear her yowling, but I can't find her.'

Twiddle remembered where she was – oh, dear, in the coal cellar! He went to the door and listened. Yes – she was yowling loudly. Then he heard another noise, too – one that puzzled him.

'Hiss-ss-ss! Hiss-ss-ss!'

'What in the world is that noise?' asked Mrs Twiddle, surprised.

'Sounds like a large snake, or something.'

'HISS-SS-SS-SS!'

'Whatever can it be?' said Mrs Twiddle
stepping back quickly. 'Gracious – if there's
an escaped snake in the garden I shall scream
the place down.'

Twiddle was just about to shut the door
when they heard another noise – a loud
cackling, angry and fierce. Mrs Twiddle
looked most alarmed.

'Why – is there a goose out in the garden
with the snake?' she asked. 'Oh, Twiddle,
dear Twiddle, I do feel frightened. Please do
go and get the dog – he'll soon scare away any

creatures that shouldn't be about.'

Twiddle was pleased to hear himself being called 'dear' again, but he didn't much like going out into the darkness among snakes and geese that seemed suddenly to have arrived from nowhere. The cat yowled loudly again.

'Let the cat in, too, wherever she is,' said Mrs Twiddle. 'Do go on, Twiddle. Aren't you brave enough?'

Twiddle didn't really think he was – but he didn't feel that he could possibly risk making Mrs Twiddle cross again, so out he went in the darkness, very valiantly.

He went to the coal-cellar and let out the cat, which flew past him and with a loud screech.

Then, hoping that he wouldn't tread on a hissing snake or bump into a fierce goose, he went to the dog's kennel. He thought that he would feel much better with the dog beside him. He opened the kennel door and called the dog.

'Come on, old fellow, come on!'

He felt a sharp pain in his hand and drew back, shocked. 'You bit me!' he said. 'You bad dog! You bit your own master! Come on out.'

But the dog wouldn't come out. Instead that peculiar hissing noise came again. Twiddle scurried away in terror.

'The snake's in the kennel with the dog – and the dog bit me!' he shouted to his wife. Mrs Twiddle was most astonished.

'The dog *bit* you!' she said. 'Our own dear gentle dog! I don't believe it. I shall go out at once with the torch and bring him in myself, snakes or no snakes!'

And out she went, shining the torch bravely in front of her. Twiddle followed her. They came to the kennel and Mrs Twiddle shone her torch in to see the dog. She gave such a loud cry of alarm and astonishment that Twiddle almost scuttled back to the house again.

'Twiddle! Look – what's this in our dog's kennel? Oh, TWIDDLE! IT'S A GOOSE!'

And sure enough an enormous goose poked out her head and cackled and hissed loudly at Mrs Twiddle. She pushed it back and shut the kennel door on it. She went back to the house with Twiddle, marvelling at the goose in the kennel.

'A goose! A *goose*! However did it get in the dog's kennel? And where is the dog? No wonder we thought there were snakes about when that goose hissed! Twiddle, did *you* put that goose into the kennel?

Twiddle was just about to say no, of course not, how could he – when a dreadful thought came into his head.

Could he *possibly* have untied a goose from that railing, instead of his dog? It had been so dark that he might have got the ropes muddled and taken someone else's goose and left his poor old dog. Yes – he remembered now – the goose had felt very soft when he had pushed what he thought was his dog, into the kennel. It must have been a goose.

He had brought back somebody's goose! Oh, dear, oh, dear!

'Maybe I brought back a goose instead of the dog,' he said. 'I stopped and had tea at a tea-room and tied the dog up outside. Now don't you say a word – I'll take back the goose and find our dog.'

So out went poor Twiddle into the rain and darkness again, pulling the surprised and angry goose behind him. How he hoped his dog was still there!

And at home Mrs Twiddle was staring angrily at the cat, who was lying on a clean cushion making it absolutely black with coal-dust from the coal-cellar! Her paws and fur were black with it.

'And where have *you* been, I should like to know?' she said. 'Sitting in the cellar again, I suppose? How many times have I chased you out of there? You bad animal! Out you go and get yourself clean in the rain!'

And when Twiddle came home with the dog he was met by the cat, flying angrily out of the door with Mrs Twiddle chasing it.

Twiddle was pleased. He never had liked his wife's cat.

'Bring the poor dog in and dry him. And dry yourself too, Twiddle.' said Mrs Twiddle in a kind voice. 'I'll make you some hot cocoa. That cat must have been in the coal-cellar again! Just *look* at my nice clean cushion!'

Twiddle looked, but he didn't say a word. He wasn't going to risk making Mrs Twiddle cross all over again by explaining how the cat got into the coal-cellar. It was nice to see her smiling once more. He and the dog could snuggle up peacefully together by the fire.

They did – and will you believe it, Twiddle is fast asleep again! And so is the dog.

Chapter 9

Mr Twiddle Gets a Surprise

'I'm just going out, my love!' Mr Twiddle
called to Mrs Twiddle.

'Twiddle! Now don't you forget the fish for
the cat!' called Mrs Twiddle, running to the
front door. 'And pay the bill at the newspaper
shop. And goodness, don't you want a basket
for the fish? You know how you make your
coat smell if you come home clutching the
packet of fish to your chest!'

'Dear me, yes – I must have a basket,' said
Twiddle. His wife ran to get it. When she
came back she had his mackintosh with her,
too. 'It's going to rain,' she said. 'You had
better take this, too, Twiddle.'

Twiddle set off, his mackintosh over one
arm, and the basket swinging in his hand. He

met Mr Grin and had a nice little talk with him. He met Miss Hurry, but she was gone before he could say more than 'Good morning'.

As he passed the cake shop a very nice smell of hot scones came out. Twiddle stopped and sniffed. 'I think I'll pop in and have a cup of hot coffee and a scone or two,' he thought. 'I really didn't have much breakfast.'

So in he went and chose a table. Soon he was sipping a cup of coffee and eating a whole plate of warm, buttered scones. Very nice, indeed!

He heard a noise outside and looked out of the window. 'There now!' he said. 'Mrs Twiddle was right – it's raining! What a good thing I've got my mac. It's simply pouring down!'

He paid his bill, picked up his basket, and went to get his mac from the peg nearby. 'Now, let me see – what did I have to get?' he wondered. 'What *was* it now? Fish for breakfast? Fetch the papers? Call at the cleaners? What shopping did I have to do?'

He struggled into his mac and went out into the rain. Bother! What was it his wife had told him to get? The rain splashed into his face, and he groped in his pocket for a handkerchief.

He brought out a nice clean one, still folded tidily. Nice Mrs Twiddle! She had even put a clean hanky in his pocket for him! He felt something else there as well, and pulled it out.

Oh, *good*! A shopping list! Now he didn't need to try and remember what he had to get. Dear Mrs Twiddle had written it all down and he couldn't possibly make a mistake! He heaved a sigh of relief.

He put his hand in the other pocket and

found his pipe there – and a small tin of his tobacco. How very, very kind of Mrs Twiddle. Mr Twiddle felt very loving towards her and made up his mind to buy her some roses. She was very fond of roses.

He lit his pipe and looked at the list of shopping. It was rather a long one – no wonder Mrs Twiddle had written it all out, instead of leaving it to him to remember! Ha – herrings for breakfast – he *thought* there was something about fish! Toothpaste – cotton wool – he must go to the chemist for those. And what was this?

'Nice big bone,' read Twiddle. 'That's a bit funny. Oh, I expect she wants it for soup. Sausages – well, I can get those at the butcher's too. And, dear me – a coal hammer! Well, well – does Mrs Twiddle expect me to break up those big lumps of coal? She hasn't said a word to me about it!'

'Chocolate cake' came next on the list. Mr Twiddle beamed. He liked chocolate cake, and Mrs Twiddle hardly ever bought one because, she said, they were too dear. And look at this – six crumpets! If there was one thing Mr Twiddle liked more than any other it was toasted crumpets for tea!

'No wonder Mrs Twiddle told me to take a basket,' he thought. 'Well, well – what a lot of shopping – but very nice shopping, I must say. Chocolate cake – crumpets – sausages. Well, I hope *those* are for supper.'

Twiddle went off happily, smoking his pipe. He must certainly remember to buy some roses for Mrs Twiddle now. After all, she was going to give him such nice meals, she deserved some roses!

He went to the fishmonger's and bought some herrings. Ha, he would enjoy those! He went to the chemist and bought his favourite toothpaste and nice big packet of cotton wool.

When he came out of the chemist's shop he found it had stopped raining, so he took off his mac and folded it neatly over his arm.

'Now to the butcher for a big bone,' said Twiddle, quite enjoying himself. 'And the sausages, too. Look at them, all looped round the front of his shop.'

He came out of the butcher's shop with two big bones and a pound of pork sausages. Then he went off to the ironmonger's and bought a really fine coal hammer. 'This will break up those big lumps of coal quite easily!'

he thought, and swung it up and down in the air.

'Now then, now then!' said a voice just behind him. 'You nearly hit me on the nose!'

It was Mr Surly, so Twiddle said he was very, very sorry, he was just trying out his coal hammer to see how it would break up big lumps of coal.

'You're lucky to *have* coal,' said Mr Surly. 'We've only got wood. And fancy having lumps big enough to break up! Where did you get them from?'

Mr Twiddle had no idea, and as he didn't at

all like Mr Surly, he popped into the shop that sold crumpets and got rid of Mr Surly that way.

He bought the biggest chocolate cake he could see and six lovely crumpets with holes in them that made them look just like flat sponges.

By this time his basket was very, very full, and he staggered homewards with it.

Last of all he bought three beautiful red roses. 'Red roses mean "I love you",' said Twiddle to himself, pleased. 'Aha! Mrs Twiddle will like those!'

He got home and went indoors. Mrs Twiddle was in the kitchen. Twiddle tiptoed into the sitting-room, got a vase, filled it with water and put the three red roses into it. He left them in the middle of the table for Mrs Twiddle to see. He called her.

'I'm in the kitchen!' she cried. 'Just baking a cake. Come in here to me, Twiddle.'

Twiddle went in with his basket. 'I've done all the shopping,' he said. 'Quite a lot, too, there was.'

'Oh, no, Twiddle dear – there wasn't very much,' said Mrs Twiddle, busy at the oven.

'Meow,' said the cat, smelling the fish and

coming over to rub herself against Mr Twiddle's legs.

'Don't,' said Twiddle. 'You make the ankles of my trousers all hairy. How many times have I told you not to do that, Cat?'

'I expect she smells the fish you've brought her,' said Mrs Twiddle, looking into her oven.

'Fish for the cat? You said herrings for breakfast!' said Twiddle, in alarm.

'I didn't!' said Mrs Twiddle. 'We've got kippers for breakfast. You bought them yourself yesterday. *Don't* say you've got herrings as well. Really, Twiddle! Did you pay the bill at the newspaper shop? I gave you the money for it.'

'Er – no. Dear me, that wasn't on the list,' said Twiddle, feeling muddled. 'Yes – I do remember your asking me now. But –'

'Oh, Twiddle! That's the second time you've forgotten to pay the bill,' said Mrs Twiddle, banging the oven door.

'Well, I remembered *everything else*,' said Twiddle. 'Here are the bones for soup – and the sausages –'

'Bones for soup? Are you mad, Twiddle?' said his little wife. 'I never said a word about bones for soup.'

'Oh, well – perhaps you wanted bones for that dog next door you're so fond of,' said Twiddle huffily. 'How was I to know? And you *did* say sausages – it was down on –'

Mrs Twiddle was now taking the things out of his basket in amazement. 'Bones – and pork sausages – and herrings. No wonder the cat was interested in your basket and came to make a fuss of you!'

She lifted out the chocolate cake and the crumpets. 'Goodness me! What in the world did you go and get these for? I *told* you I was baking cakes today! Twiddle, I really begin to think you've gone mad!'

She took out the toothpaste and the cotton wool. 'Ah look at these! You had a new tube of toothpaste yesterday – and, why all this cotton wool? Are you going to stuff a cushion or something? And TWIDDLE! Is that a coal hammer? Oh, Twiddle, you'll be the death of me! You know we haven't any coal – only a bit of coke and some wood!'

'Well,' began Twiddle, most annoyed, 'all these things were down on your –'

'Twiddle! You must have spent all the money I gave you for the newspaper bill on these things!' said Mrs Twiddle. 'It was my house-keeping money! It was very wrong of you to do that. You can pay for them all out of your own money!'

Twiddle was most alarmed. 'But I can't. I only have enough to . . .'

Mrs Twiddle burst into tears. 'Why did you get all those things? Now I shall never, *never* be able to trust you to go shopping again.'

There came a knock at the front door just then. Twiddle went to see who it was, feeling very gloomy indeed. A tall man stood there, dressed in a mackintosh. He beamed at Twiddle.

'I say,' he said, 'I'm very, very sorry – but I've done something so silly.'

Twiddle was very, very glad to hear that someone else could do silly things. He asked the man in at once. 'It's like this,' said the man, standing in the hall, 'I went to have a cup of coffee at the tea shop – and by mistake I took your mac when I went out. So I've brought it back. It had your name in it. Did you by any chance take mine? They are alike!'

Mrs Twiddle came out to hear what all the talking was about. She looked at the mac Twiddle had hung in the hall. 'Yes – he took yours!' she said. 'They *are* alike! Dear, dear – you men!'

'Good gracious!' said Twiddle, light dawning on him all at once. 'I smoked your pipe, then – and used your hanky – and oh, my word, I bought all the things on your shopping list!'

'No! Did you really?' said the tall man. 'You know, I tried to remember everything that was down, but I couldn't. I bought the chocolate cake and the crumpets – and I bought the bones for soup, and the sausages and the herrings. Was there anything else on the list?'

'Yes – toothpaste – cotton wool – and a coal hammer,' said Twiddle dolefully.

'My word!' said the man. 'I forgot all those. I *shall* get into trouble when I get back home. But do you *want* toothpaste and cotton wool and a coal hammer?'

'Of course not!' said Mrs Twiddle, answering for Twiddle. 'You can have them if you'd like to pay us for them.'

'Oh, I will, with pleasure,' said the man. 'It will save me going back to the shops. Dear, dear – I must have the worst memory in the world.'

'Yes – even worse than mine,' agreed Twiddle happily 'Here's the hammer – toothpaste – and cotton wool.'

'I'm sorry you bought the other things,' said the man, paying out the money. 'But I've bought them, too, and I really couldn't face my wife with *two* chocolate cakes, *two* lots of sausages, *two* –'

'No, no, of course not,' said Twiddle, who was not at all anxious to hand over the cake, the crumpets and the rest.

The man took off Twiddle's mac, and Twiddle gave him the right one. They said goodbye, and out he went, his basket full.

Mrs Twiddle still looked very cross. Twiddle knew she had a lot more to say.

'Come into the sitting-room, Twiddle,' said Mrs Twiddle, in a stern voice. 'I have something to say to you.' He followed her in, feeling very gloomy. She suddenly saw the three red roses in the vase.

'Wherever did those lovely flowers come from?' said Mrs Twiddle, and sniffed them in delight.

'I bought them for you,' said Twiddle, in a small voice.

'Red roses mean "I love you,"' said Mrs Twiddle, her eyes shining.

'That's why I bought them,' said Twiddle. 'I may be a very silly husband, but I do think you are a nice wife. So I bought you those roses.'

'Twiddle, you're a darling!' said Mrs Twiddle, and she gave him a very sudden hug. 'Now, when would you like the sausages? For supper? And I'll make some nice soup with those bones. And herrings will do fine for breakfast, because the kippers will keep. And we'll have a little tea party with those lovely crumpets and chocolate cake!'

Well, well, well! Twiddle simply couldn't

understand the sudden change. But I can, can't you? After all, if somebody loves you very much, you can put up with quite a lot of silliness! Dear old Twiddle, I can't help liking him.